Toby:

We'll have fun
reading this to-
gether. *
        *

Love
Grandma
9/24/92

SESAME STREET

SILLY STORIES™

Oscar's Silly ABC's

and Other Stories

By Michaela Muntean
Illustrated by Tom Brannon

Featuring Jim Henson's Sesame Street Muppets

A Sesame Street/Golden Press Book

Published by Western Publishing Company, Inc., in conjunction
with Children's Television Workshop

Oscar's Silly ABC's

Every Grouch should know lots of words for insults, grumbling, and general grouchiness. Grouches also like words that sound silly. The ABC's of grouchery can be found in the official *Grumpster's Dictionary*. In case you don't have a copy in your garbage can, Oscar has selected an alphabet of his favorite grouchy and silly words for you.

abominable   Awful; terrible.

The abominable snow monster is not the sort of monster these monsters would like to meet.

bumblebee   A flying insect. Some bumblebees sting.

A bumblebee is buzzing around Betty Lou as she picks a bunch of buttercups.

cantankerous   Bad-tempered; cranky.

Grouches get very cantankerous when they find flowers growing in their crabgrass gardens.

disgusting   Sickening.

Ernie thinks that Oscar's chocolate-covered sardine sundae looks disgusting.

exit   To leave. The way out.

A Grouch is an expert at showing visitors the exit.

flabbergasted   Very surprised.

glob   A lump or pile of something

Farley is flabbergasted when he sees the glob of mashed turnips on Ferdinand's plate.

hippopotamus   A large animal with a big head, short legs, and thick skin.

A hippopotamus will never fit on a bus.

ch   A feeling that makes you want to scratch.

Oscar has an itch in the middle of his back.

ggling   An uneven bumping or bouncing motion.

angaroo   An animal that can leap and hop on its back legs. A mother kangaroo carries her baby in a pouch.

The baby kangaroo is jiggling up and down in his mother's pouch.

lollipop   A piece of hard candy on a stick.

Leo's lollipop is stuck to his fur.

macaroni   A tube-shaped noodle.

Oscar is making macaroni and marshmallows for lunch.

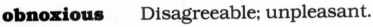

nuisance   A pest.

Oscar's nephew, Nestor, makes a nuisance of himself by asking for a new piece of junk every few minutes.

obnoxious   Disagreeable; unpleasant.

Oscar is obnoxious when the kids are jumping rope.

porcupine   A small animal covered with stiff sharp quills.

Some Grouches like to have porcupines for pets.

uiet   Silence; no noise.

If everyone would quit talking,
we could have some peace
and quiet around here!

rotten   Spoiled; stinky.

Stinkweed smells and tastes rotten,
and Grouches love it.

crumptious   Very tasty; delicious.

A sardine sandwich on a
soggy sesame-seed bun is
simply scrumptious!

tickle   A light touch that
makes you want to
laugh.

Ernie is going to tickle Bert
with a feather.

ukelele   A small four-stringed musical instrument.

vamoose   Go away; scram!

I wish you and that ukelele would vamoose!

wiggle   To move from side to side.

Oscar's pet worm, Slimey, can wiggle when he walks.

xylophone   A musical instrument made of wooden bars and played with two small wooden mallets.

Xavier plays the xylophone at exactly eight o'clock every day.

o-yo A toy that goes up and down on a string.

The Count is counting how many times Grover's yo-yo is going up and down.

zipper Something that is used to fasten clothes or other things together.

Herry is trying to zip up the zipper on his jacket.

"That's it," Oscar says. "Twenty-six silly words, one for each letter from A to Z. Now it's time for *you* to vamoose! Good-bye, and have a really rotten Grouch day!"

Snuggle Up with a Snuffle-upagus

A Snuffle-upagus is big and warm and furry. He has a long snuffle, which comes in very handy for carrying things and for giving his friends a hug.

Snuffle-upaguses are kind and thoughtful. They always remember to send thank-you notes and to return their library books on time. But one of the nicest things about Snuffle-upaguses is that they are very snuggly.

If the day is dark and rainy, and your galoshes go
slishity-slosh through the puddles and *squishity-squash*
through the mud…

If the wind is whistling a nasty tune, and it's a gloomy
afternoon…

Hurry home and snuggle up with a Snuffle-upagus.
He'll keep you warm and dry.

If you have the measles or mumps, or are down in the dumps…

If you hear a squeak and a creak and you can't go to sleep…

Snuggle up with a Snuffle-upagus. He's sure to cheer you up-agus!

Amazing Word Tricks

A hush falls over the crowd as the curtain goes up. The Amazing Mumford, with his assistant, Grover, at his side, is about to perform some amazing word tricks.

For his first trick the Amazing Mumford shows the audience the word ROCK.

"By changing only *one* letter," he says, "I will make a completely new word. Are you ready?"

Everyone is wondering what will happen when the Amazing Mumford says the words A LA PEANUT BUTTER SANDWICHES! In a flash the word ROCK has become the word SOCK! Isn't that amazing?

The Amazing Mumford will now add *two* letters to the word PAN to change it into a new word. The letters he will add will be a T and an S.

The people in the audience are on the edge of their seats, wondering what the new word will be. Mumford says the magic words, and with a flash and a crash, PAN becomes PANTS! What a wonderful word trick!

For his next trick the Amazing Mumford will begin with the little word KEY. This time he will add *three* letters to make a brand-new word.

With a flash and a crash and a bip-boom-bash, the word KEY becomes TURKEY. The audience is absolutely astonished!

For his last and most difficult trick the Amazing Mumford pulls six letters out of his magic hat. The letters are: two E's, one T, one H, one N, and one D. Everyone knows that EETHND is not a word, but that does not worry the Amazing Mumford.

"A LA PEANUT BUTTER SANDWICHES!" he cries. After an enormous flash and a crash and a bip-boom-bash, we see that EETHND spells

THE END.